Time Jumpers

DODGING DINOSAURS

by
WENDY MASS

illustrated by
ORIOL VIDAL

BRANCHES
SCHOLASTIC INC.

Read all the Time Jumpers adventures!

scholastic.com/timejumpers

Table of Contents

1: Hold On to Your Hat! 1

2: Back to the Museum 6

3: The Adventure Begins! 11

4: Stampede! 17

5: Go Climb a Tree! 24

6: Stop Bugging Me! 28

7: Hold On! 34

8: Help Is Here 41

9: Finn's Tale 46

10: Crack! 50

11: Red to the Rescue! 55

12: Are You My Mother? 62

13: An Unexpected Visitor 67

14: Frenemies 72

15: A Dino Is Born 80

16: Dinos and Donuts 85

For Mike, for traveling through time

with me! — WM

For all dinosaur lovers. You will enjoy

this one! — OV

Text copyright © 2019 by Wendy Mass
Illustrations by Oriol Vidal copyright © 2019 by Scholastic Inc.

Library of Congress Cataloging-in-Publication Data

Names: Mass, Wendy, 1967- author. | Vidal, Oriol, 1977- illustrator. | Mass, Wendy, 1967- Time jumpers ; 4.
Title: Dodging dinosaurs / by Wendy Mass ; illustrated by Oriol Vidal.
Description: First edition. | New York, NY : Branches/Scholastic Inc., 2019.
Series: Time jumpers ; 4 | Summary: On a visit to the Natural History Museum, Chase and Ava seem on the verge of finding out something important about the mysterious Randall, the missing scientist Finn, and the woman who gave them the suitcase filled with magical objects, when the dinosaur egg from the suitcase (they thought it was a potato) sends them back to dinosaur times—where they have to return the egg to the correct brontosaurus nest, while eluding hungry dinosaurs, and Randall, who it turns out is working for somebody called The Collector.
Identifiers: LCCN 2018053888| ISBN 9781338217452 (pbk) | ISBN 9781338217469 (hardcover)
Subjects: LCSH: Time travel—Juvenile fiction. | Dinosaurs—Juvenile fiction. | Magic—Juvenile fiction. | Brothers and sisters—Juvenile fiction. | Adventure stories. | CYAC: Time travel—Fiction. | Dinosaurs—Fiction. | Magic—Fiction. | Brothers and sisters—Fiction. | Adventure and adventurers—Fiction. | LCGFT: Action and adventure fiction.
Classification: LCC PZ7.M42355 Do 2019 | DDC 813.54 [Fic]
—dc23 LC record available at https://lccn.loc.gov/2018053888

10 9 8 7 6 5 4 3 2 1   19 20 21 22 23

Printed in China   62
First edition, August 2019
Illustrated by Oriol Vidal
Edited by Katie Carella
Book design by Sunny Lee

Hold On to Your Hat!

chapter 1

Knock-knock.

Chase yawns as his eyes slowly open. He's lying on a hard, wooden floor, with his sister Ava's foot an inch from his nose.

For a few seconds he's not sure where they are. In King Arthur's castle? A tomb in Egypt? Or are they one hundred years in the future? He and Ava have been to all those amazing places in the last few days.

As soon as he sits up, Chase knows they're in his bedroom. He can't believe they'd taken a nap in the middle of the afternoon, but they'd barely slept in days.

"Kids?" Mom's voice calls from the hall.

"Wake up," Chase whispers to Ava. "Mom is coming!"

Her eyes snap open. "The suitcase!"

Their suitcase is still wide open on the floor! A woman named Madeline  gave it to them at the flea market a few days ago. Any time they touch one of the strange objects inside, they're sent traveling through time. They can't get home until they return the object to its rightful place in history. This would be easier to do if they weren't being chased by a man named Randall who wants the items back.

Ava pushes the suitcase with her foot. It skids under the bed. They yelp as two items pop out—the remote control that has sent them home each time and the uncooked potato, which is bouncing up and down!

Chase's doorknob begins to turn. The bedroom door is opening!

Chase tosses his baseball cap on top of the items just as Mom's head appears.

"Are you two up for a trip to the museum?" she asks. "There's a new planetarium show that Dad and I would like to see."

Chase and Ava both nod excitedly. The Natural History Museum is *exactly* where they want to go! Madeline's uncle Finn used to work there. He was the original owner of the suitcase, and they have *lots* of questions for him. Hopefully someone at the museum can tell them where he went.

"Let's go then," Mom says.

Chase can't return the remote and the potato to the suitcase without their mom seeing. And he can't risk touching them and disappearing either. He has no choice but to gather them up under his hat. Guess they're coming along for the ride!

chapter 2

Back to the Museum

Thankfully, they arrive at the museum without Chase suddenly disappearing from the car!

Chase and Ava have been visiting this museum since they were in strollers. They would always stop to see the huge brontosaurus skeleton in the lobby. But during their time jump into the future, they'd discovered that the brontosaurus had mysteriously been replaced by a stegosaurus. Sure enough, when they walk inside now, it's the stegosaurus that greets them. It's a cool dinosaur, but it's not the *right* dinosaur. Where did the brontosaurus go?

Still clutching his hat, Chase asks his parents, "Do you guys remember the huge brontosaurus that used to be here?"

They both shake their heads. "This has always been a stegosaurus," Dad says. "Wait here while we get the schedule for the planetarium."

When they leave, Ava asks, "How come we're the only people who remember the brontosaurus?"

"Time jumpers must be able to tell when something has changed in the present," Chase suggests. "Come on, let's go find out where Madeline's uncle Finn went. Maybe he'll know more."

A tour is gathering near them. The tour guide's badge says I'M JESSICA, ASK ME ANYTHING!

"Do you know a guy who used to work here named Finn?" Chase asks her.

Jessica nods. "Finn is one of our best scientists. I think the museum sent him on a long vacation though. He'd been acting strangely. Going on about a missing dinosaur."

"A man named Randall told us Finn had been fired," Chase says.

Jessica shakes her head. "Nope."

"Do you know Randall?" Ava asks. "He works here, too. He's tall, two different-colored eyes, shiny head, always mean?"

"Sorry. No one like that works here." Jessica turns back to her tour group.

"That's weird," Chase whispers to Ava. "We *know* Randall works here. We saw him use his employee badge after our Egyptian adventure."

But Ava is no longer listening. She's pointing at a nearby poster. "That dinosaur egg looks exactly like our potato!"

Chase opens his hat to peek inside. The potato tries to jump out! Chase quickly clasps it shut again.

"Ava," he says in a shaky voice. "This isn't a potato. It's a DINOSAUR EGG!"

The Adventure Begins!

chapter 3

"We have a *real* dinosaur egg?" Ava asks, peering at the object in Chase's hat. "Like the kind that would hatch a real DINOSAUR?"

"I think so," Chase says.

A janitor sweeping nearby waves them over. "Hi. I'm Tom. I overheard you asking about Finn and Randall?"

Chase nods. "Do you know them?"

"Jessica was right about Randall not working here," Tom confirms. "But he does come to the museum a lot. His job is to sell interesting objects. I don't think Finn's on vacation though."

"Then where is he?" Ava asks.

"I don't know," Tom says, lowering his voice. "A few months ago I was cleaning outside his office when I heard him and Randall arguing. This was around the time Finn had started acting strangely — arguing with everyone about that dinosaur in the lobby. Anyway, I heard Randall accuse him of stealing something of his."

"The suitcase, I bet!" Ava whispers to Chase.

"Then Randall stormed out," Tom adds. "When I went in to clean Finn's office, he wasn't  there. So either Finn slipped past me or he disappeared into thin air."

Chase and Ava gulp. They know a little something about disappearing into thin air.

"Can we check out Finn's office?" Chase asks Tom. "Maybe something there will tell us where he went."

"It's down that hallway," Tom tells them, pointing. "Good luck." Then he goes back to sweeping.

Chase and Ava rejoin their parents. "Would it be okay if Ava and I skip the planetarium?" Chase asks them.

"Are you sure?" Dad asks. "They're going to hand out donuts to represent the rings of Saturn."

Ava's eyes light up at the mention of dessert.

Chase grabs her sleeve. "We really want to hear the dinosaur tour," he says.

"All right," Mom says. "Stick together and meet us afterward at the information booth."

Chase and Ava follow the tour for a bit, then duck into the hallway marked STAFF OFFICES.

Chase grabs the two smallest tour guide uniforms off the wall. "These will help us blend in." He and Ava slip them over their clothes.

Finn's office is easy to find. They quickly slip inside.

A framed photo of Madeline sits on the desk. She has her arm around a man with a beard. They're both smiling.

"That man must be Finn," Ava guesses.

Chase starts to nod, then says, "Uh-oh!" The egg has started moving around so forcefully he can barely hold on to his hat. It bursts out of the hat and flies into the air! It's about to crash down on the desk!

Ava lunges for the egg and catches it! Chase grabs her other hand and slips the remote into his pocket just as the office begins to spin.

The museum disappears behind them.

chapter 4

Stampede!

The feeling of spinning through time lasts much longer than usual. Finally, Chase and Ava land splayed out on a hot, mossy field.

Chase can hardly believe what he's seeing. Next to ancient Egypt, prehistoric times are his favorite historical period. They just traveled back in time over a *hundred million years*!

Suddenly, the ground begins to rumble and shake! In the distance, a giant plume of dust rises into the air.

"What's that?" Ava asks, her eyes wide with fear.

The dust clears for a second, long enough for Chase to see behind it. He gasps. "Ava! DINOSAURS!"

"We're going to get trampled!" Ava shouts. The dinosaurs thundering toward them range from the size of a car to the size of their *house*!

The ground begins to shake harder as the herd closes in. Chase stuffs the egg into his pocket.

He and Ava dart into a nearby grove of trees. These trees aren't like the ones in their yard at home with low branches that make them easy to climb. These look more like palm trees with skinny leaves.

They have to climb to safety though! They dig their fingertips into the bark and scamper up the trunk, holding on tight as the tree shakes and bends from their weight.

The herd rushes past them. Some of the dinosaurs have scales, some have feathers, and some are smooth. Chase knows meat eaters like the Tyrannosaurus rex run on two legs, but these dinosaurs all seem to have four legs. Phew!

Ava points to a small reddish dinosaur with little spikes on its body. "That's a dicraeosaurus!" Chase says.

"He might be a baby dinosaur," Ava whispers. She snaps a picture from her camera as the small red dinosaur passes by, much slower than the others.

None of the dinosaurs had even turned in their direction.

"If those dinosaurs weren't after *us*," Ava says, "then why were they running?"

"Something must've scared them," Chase replies.

Just then, a creature that looks like a giant lizard runs up to the base of their tree.

The creature sniffs the air. Then it opens its mouth wide and, with rows of pointy teeth, takes a giant bite out of the trunk! Chase is so surprised that he loses his grip and begins to slide down the trunk right toward it!

Go Climb a Tree!

chapter 5

"Hang on, Chase!" Ava yells. She grabs her brother's collar and yanks him back up on the tree. She always has been unusually strong for her size.

"Go away!" she shouts at the creature.

With a whimper, the giant lizard slinks off.

Ava grins. "I showed *him* who's boss!"

Chase points up at the sky. "I'm pretty sure *that guy*'s the boss." Circling only inches above the treetop is what looks like a winged dinosaur!

Ava shrinks back. "What kind of dinosaur is *that*?"

"It's not a dinosaur. It is a prehistoric reptile called a pterosaur," Chase says. "It's basically a giant lizard with wings."

The pterosaur gets *so* close that one wing grazes Ava's hair! She squeals.

Chase quickly scans the ground to make sure the lizard creature hasn't returned. "We need to get out of this tree," he says. "That pterosaur probably has eggs in a nest up there that it's protecting."

"Maybe *our* egg is supposed to be in that nest!" Ava says. "Once we return it, maybe it will hatch into the dinosaur it was always meant to become."

The pterosaur squawks angrily.

The dinosaur it was always meant to become, Chase repeats in his head. "That's it!" he exclaims. "You're a genius, Ava! Our egg is not a pterosaur egg. But I know *exactly* who our egg will become!"

He slides down the tree trunk.

"I think the prehistoric heat has fried your brain," Ava says, sliding down after him. "How could you know who it will become?"

"Think about it, Ava," Chase says as they hurry back to the field. "There's only one dinosaur we know of that has disappeared."

Chase sees understanding dawn on her face. At the same time, they say, "The missing brontosaurus from the museum!"

chapter 6

Stop Bugging Me!

"Pulling the egg out of time meant it never got a chance to hatch," Chase says. "That's why a different dinosaur is at the museum now."

"So there are two timelines for this egg. One where it hatched, the dinosaur lived a full life, and its bones ended up on display at the museum. And one where the egg was stolen out of time, so a different dinosaur skeleton ended up there?"

"Exactly," Chase replies.

"Finn must remember both timelines, like we do," Ava says. "That's why he was arguing with the rest of the staff. He knew the brontosaurus was missing even if no one else did. I wish we could talk to him and let him know he's not crazy."

"The sooner we find out where this brontosaurus egg belongs," Chase says, "the sooner we'll get home to find Finn."

The sun beat down on them as they trudged across the open field.

"I'm soooo thirsty," Ava says. "And I'd love a chocolate ice-cream cone."

"I can't help with the ice cream," Chase says, "but I spotted a stream when we were up in the tree."

They hear the babbling of the stream before they get there. By the time they reach it, the sky has clouded over.

"Look!" Ava points downstream. "We aren't the only thirsty ones!"

The small red dinosaur they saw earlier is there, flicking a flying insect with its tail. Chase glances around to make sure no larger dinosaurs are nearby.

"Let's call him Red!" Ava says. "I want to get a picture."

"Wait!" Chase calls out, but she's already running along the stream.

The sudden movement catches Red's attention. He takes a step toward her. Ava freezes! But Red just nuzzles her hand.

"That was really dangerous," Chase says when he catches up.

"I'm sorry," Ava says. But since Red is now resting his chin on Ava's hand and gazing up at her lovingly, the apology doesn't sound very heartfelt.

"Ouch!" Chase says, slapping at his neck. "Something bit me!" A drop of blood comes off on his hand! He looks around to see a HUGE flying insect. Like, fifty times the size of mosquitoes back home, with a stinger the length of a human hand!

A loud buzzing fills the air. The gigantic insect has *friends*!

chapter 7

Hold On!

A swarm of the huge insects fills the air!

Chase and Ava run, waving their arms to fend off the insects. They reach the open field just as it begins to rain.

Thankfully the bugs fly back into the protection of the trees, but Chase and Ava have to find cover from the storm!

"Over here," Chase says, ducking under a rock ledge. They huddle underneath, watching the rain turn the ground to mud.

"This rain is making me even thirstier," Ava says.

The rainwater slides down the long leaves of the nearby plants, giving Chase an idea. He reaches out and pulls off two of the longest leaves.

He gives one to Ava and says, "Watch." He bends the leaf until it looks like an open hot dog bun, and holds it 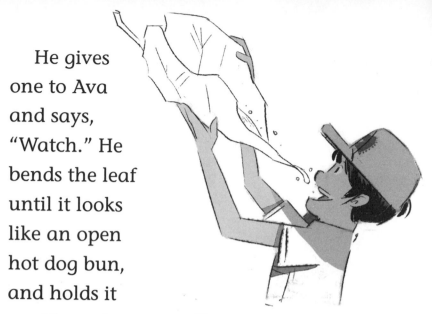 up. The rainwater collects inside. He tilts the leaf toward himself, and the water pours into his mouth. "Ahh, refreshing!"

Ava laughs and does the same thing with her leaf. They drink until it stops raining.

"We still have to find something to eat. And don't say *ice cream* again," Chase says. "Red is an herbivore, so he eats mostly plants and fruits. Whatever he eats should be safe for us, too."

"Let's go!" Ava says.

On the way to find Red, Ava makes a giant flyswatter out of a twig and some leaves. She waves it around like a sword, shouting, "Crazy, giant prehistoric mosquitoes, you've met your match!"

They find Red downstream, chomping on what looks like a long pinecone. Chase can see Red's rows of jagged teeth as they slice through the snack.

Ava tucks her flyswatter into her belt and frowns. "That pinecone doesn't look very tasty. What about these berries?" She points to purple berries on a bush.

"Let's see if Red will eat them." Chase plucks a few and holds them out to Red.

Red gobbles them up.

Chase grins. He just fed a dinosaur!

Chase and Ava pop the berries into their mouths. Yum! They fill their pockets and head out in search of the right nest for their egg. Chase takes the lead, trying to avoid the mud puddles.

From a few feet behind, Ava calls out, "What does a dinosaur nest even look like? Is it—"

Chase turns around. "Is it *what*?"

Ava is standing still. "Chase!" she says in a shaky voice. "My feet are stuck!"

Chase watches in horror as his sister begins to sink into the ground! First her legs, then up to her waist! She flails her arms, which only makes her sink faster.

Quicksand! He's read about it but never thought he'd see it in real life! If he ran to her they'd both be stuck. The only thing Chase can think of is to grab a fallen tree branch and hold it out to her. But instead of him pulling *her* out with the branch, she's pulling *him* toward the quicksand!

Chase's heart thunders in his chest. The sand is up to Ava's armpits! The suction of the quicksand is too strong! He'll never get her out!

Help Is Here

chapter 8

Two arms circle around Chase's waist and tug him backward.

Chase's brain can't process what's happening. There were no humans in prehistoric times! Is a *dinosaur* helping him rescue Ava? But he can see old tattered shirtsleeves on the arms around his waist and DINOSAURS DON'T WEAR CLOTHES.

Either way, the extra force is working. Ava is rising out of the quicksand!

At last she is able to climb out. She lets go of the branch and flops on the ground, breathing hard.

Chase rushes to her side. "Are you okay?"

Ava nods, and then she starts laughing and wiping away tears. "Well, that was terrifying!"

Chase gives her a hug. "Yeah, let's not do that again."

Only then do they turn around to see who had helped them. A man, about sixty years old, is sitting on a large rock. He is deeply tanned with a scraggly beard.

Their jaws fall open! They've seen him before, although he looks different from the framed picture on his desk.

"*Finn*?" they say at the same time.

"That's me," he replies. Then he looks at Chase's hat. "And you must be Chase and Ava Teslar. I can't tell you how happy I am to see you."

Their jaws fall open again. "You *know* us?" Ava asks.

"Well, technically I know Chase," Finn says as he turns to Chase. "Years ago, you were on a school field trip and you impressed me with your dinosaur knowledge. You told me both your names when I gave you that hat."

Chase's eyes widen. So *Finn* had been the scientist who gave him his favorite hat! "That was you?"

Finn nods. "My parents told me bedtime stories about time jumpers. They said a brother and sister would come to my rescue one day, but I thought they were just spinning tales to help me sleep. Now I think you two *must* be the time jumpers from their stories. And I'm almost certain my parents must have been time jumpers themselves."

"Madeline told us about that story!" Chase says.

"Are you a time jumper, too?" Ava asks eagerly.

"I was hoping *you* could tell me that," Finn replies.

"We don't know much about time travel, even though we've done it a lot now," Ava says. "We were hoping *you* would be able to explain it to *us*."

"I'm sorry," Finn says. "All I can tell you for sure is what happened to me." He draws a deep breath. Chase and Ava move closer. This is going to be a good story!

chapter 9

Finn's Tale

Finn paces as he talks. "Part of my job at the museum is to look for new items to add to our collections. A man named Randall used to come in with old clay pots and arrowheads, small things like that. Then he started hinting that soon he'd have more *interesting* items for sale."

Chase and Ava hang on every word as Finn goes on. "Randall would slink around the museum with his suitcase, acting suspicious. One day he left the suitcase in the coat-check room, and I couldn't help it. I *had* to peek. It was full of strange objects, including a dinosaur egg. I couldn't believe it! I reached a finger out to touch the egg, certain it couldn't be real. I quickly pulled my hand back, but it was too late.

Suddenly, I was hovering in the air in prehistoric times! That's when I *knew* that my parents' time jumper stories were real. A minute later I was back in the coat-check room."

Chase remembered how he'd gotten a glimpse of Egypt when his finger grazed the jeweled beetle. That's how they'd learned that time jumpers had to be fully holding an object to land somewhere. A slight touch would only let you get a fast glimpse of the place.

"You're definitely a time jumper," Chase says. "You could open the suitcase, which regular people can't. You traveled when you touched one of the objects inside. And you remember *both* timelines — the one where the brontosaurus was in the museum, and the one where it wasn't. We're pretty sure only time jumpers can do those things."

"You must be right," Finn says.

"What happened next?" Ava asks.

"I knew the objects in the suitcase must've been stolen, so I snatched it and ran," Finn replies. "I gave it to my niece, Madeline, to hold on to until I could figure out what was going on. How did you two end up with it?"

Ava tells him about how Madeline gave them the suitcase at the flea market, and how Randall has been chasing them through time to get it back.

Then Chase reaches into his pocket and holds out the egg. "I think you'll be happy to see this."

chapter 10

Crack!

"The egg from the suitcase!" Finn exclaims, cradling it in his hands.

Ava frowns. "I don't understand how you landed here, Finn. How did you get to prehistoric times without the egg?"

"When Randall discovered his suitcase was missing, he stormed into my office," Finn tells them. "He pulled what I thought was a phone from his pocket, and I grabbed for it before he could call anyone. But it was a remote control. We fought over it and I pushed one of its buttons by accident. Before I even knew what happened, I was swirling in circles. I've been here ever since. I've learned more about prehistoric times in my ten days here than in thirty years of research!"

Ava glances at Chase, then says, "Um, it's been four months since you disappeared."

Finn's eyes widen. "What?"

"Time jumping is weird like that," Chase explains. "You'll get used to it."

Finn shakes his head in amazement. "I guess I'll have to! Now let's put this brontosaurus egg back where it belongs." He hands it to Chase. "You got it this far."

But as soon as he says it, a crack forms right down the middle of the egg! Finn leans in for a closer look. "It's going to hatch soon," he declares.

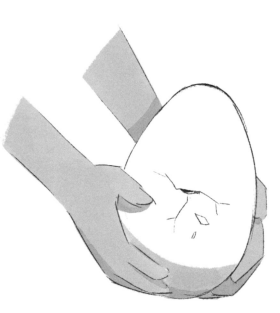

"We can't let it hatch here," Chase explains to Finn, tucking it away again. "We have to return it to the exact spot where it was taken from or else we'll be trapped in prehistoric times forever."

"But how will we ever find where it belongs?" Ava asks.

"Dinosaurs sometimes lay their eggs in a line as they walk," Finn says. "We'll look for a break in a line of eggs. I've been tracking a herd of brontosauruses. They're the largest breed out here, so they're easy to spot."

They take off running along the edge of the woods. A minute later Finn's arms shoot out in front of Chase and Ava.

A huge two-legged dinosaur is running right at them!

Red to the Rescue!

chapter 11

The two-legged dinosaur sprinting toward them has a single horn in the middle of its face and long pointy teeth sticking out of its mouth.

"Is that a ceratosaurus?" Chase cries.

"Yes! Good eye, Chase!" Finn says, herding them back into the woods. "We don't want to mess with that guy. Follow me!"

Finn weaves in and out of trees. Chase and Ava are getting good at dodging dinosaurs!

The ceratosaurus knocks down trees left and right as it chases them.

"I'll go this way, you go the other," Finn calls back to Chase and Ava.

Finn bolts left, waving his arms to draw attention to himself.

But the ceratosaurus stays focused on Chase and Ava. It is closing in fast!

"Keep running!" Finn shouts. He doubles back and tries to distract the dinosaur by tossing rocks at it. But the rocks only make the dinosaur growl.

Suddenly, Red appears behind Chase and Ava! The small dinosaur runs right into the charging ceratosaurus, knocking it over!

Then Red takes off.

The ceratosaurus scrambles to its feet and darts after him, roaring as it goes. Red can't run very fast on his stubby legs, but he had a good head start.

Finn catches his breath and smiles. "I can always count on Red."

Chase and Ava laugh. "We call him Red, too," Ava says. "Will he be okay?"

"I am sure he will," Finn assures them. "Many dinosaurs have such small brains that my fellow scientists always thought they weren't very bright. But we sure got that wrong!"

They walk back to the large field without any more scary encounters. Finn points to a group of brontosauruses nibbling on a clump of trees in the distance.

"Those dinos are enormous!" Ava says.

Finn nods. "Brontosauruses are one of the largest plant-eating dinosaurs."

The sun has begun to set behind the dinosaurs. "Isn't that a beautiful sight," Finn says with a sigh. Ava already has her camera out.

"Look!" Chase says, pointing to a row of eggs on the ground near the brontosauruses.

They tiptoe forward to get a closer look. There's definitely a large gap between two of the eggs. "That must be where our egg belongs!" Chase exclaims. He can feel the egg rattling harder in his pocket. Time's almost up!

chapter 12

Are You My Mother?

Finn, Chase, and Ava get as close to the line of eggs as they dare.

Two brontosauruses are pacing up and down the line like they're standing guard. "Those must be the moms," Finn whispers. "They're protecting the eggs from predators. Any of the meat eaters could snatch one right up."

One brontosaurus begins walking in circles, her head low. "I bet that's our egg's mom," Chase whispers. "She seems sad, and it looks like she's searching for something."

The mom lifts her head, looks right at them, and grunts. They've been spotted! The whole herd starts moving slowly toward them, away from their eggs. And a few brontosauruses whip their tails, causing a loud cracking sound.

Soon Chase, Ava, and Finn are all surrounded.

The brontosauruses tower over them, taller than any of the trees. The mom bends her long neck down until she is almost eye to eye with Chase! He's excited to be *so* close to a real dinosaur, but he can't stop his hands from shaking. The mom is  HUGE and very strong. And she could use a breath mint. Maybe a *box* of breath mints.

The circle gets tighter around them. Chase's heart speeds up as tails whip through the air, coming dangerously close to smacking them. Ava whimpers. The egg in Chase's pocket shakes even harder.

A flash of light outside the circle catches their attention. Through the brontosauruses' legs they see a most unlikely sight: a tall man in a beekeeper outfit holding a large duffel bag. The man takes off the beekeeper mask and the setting sun glints off his head.

Chase's stomach twists. He knows who this is!

An Unexpected Visitor

"Randall!" Chase and Ava exclaim at the same time. With all the other dangerous things here to look out for, they hadn't even thought about Randall. They should have known he'd show up.

The circle of brontosauruses continues to close in around them and Finn.

"Randall!" Finn shouts across the field. "You need to help us!"

Chase whispers to Ava, "If Finn thinks Randall is going to help us, he's nuts."

Randall's duffel bag slips from his shoulder and lands with a *thud*.

The sound catches the brontosauruses' attention. They turn toward him, growling and swishing their tails.

Randall reaches into the bag. He pulls out a large horn and blows into it.

BRUUUP!!

Chase and Ava cover their ears. The dinosaurs scatter! The mom lingers the longest but finally slinks away, too.

"Thank you," Finn calls out to Randall.

Chase is pretty sure Randall only helped them because he was in danger himself. Still, he's glad not to be surrounded by angry dinosaurs anymore.

"Can we put the egg back now?" Ava whispers to Chase. "The dinosaurs are gone."

Chase glances over at the empty spot in the line of eggs and shakes his head. "Randall is too close. He's tried to stop us each time we've tried to return an object. We can't let him get this egg."

Randall marches toward them. "Too bad we're not on the same side," he snaps. "I could really use a time jumper as a partner. Then I wouldn't need this annoying remote to travel anywhere."

"How come your remote works differently from ours?" Ava asks.

Not surprisingly, Randall ignores her. He sees Finn eyeing the remote and quickly tucks it into his duffel bag. "Don't get any ideas about trapping me here."

"Like *you* trapped *me* here?" Finn says, hands on his hips.

"That wasn't on purpose," Randall insists. "*You* pressed the button. I had no idea where you went when you disappeared."

Finn opens his mouth to argue, then shuts it. "Let's just let the kids replace the egg. Then we can all go home."

"I can't let them do that. You don't understand," Randall says. But before he can explain further, a buzzing fills the air. The giant stinging insects are back!

chapter 14

Frenemies

Randall shoves his beekeeper mask back on.

"Ouch!" Finn shouts as an insect's long stinger grazes his arm.

Chase covers his head. "Get low, Ava!" he calls to her.

"One sec," she says, pulling her giant flyswatter out of her belt.

She waves it wildly in the air to try to keep the huge insects away from them. It's helping, but it's not enough.

"You time jumpers really need to be more prepared," Randall says, yanking a battery-operated fan out of his bag.

He turns it on and blows the insects backward. They fly off.

Ava turns to Chase. "That time, I think Randall really *did* help us," she says.

Randall hears her and grumbles, "Don't get used to it." He stashes the fan back in the duffel.

Ava peers into his bag. "Do you have any snacks in there?"

Randall reaches for the bag's zipper to close it, but before he can grasp on to it, Finn slips his hand into the bag and grabs the remote control!

Randall's eyes go wide as he realizes what has happened.

Finn backs away from Randall, holding Randall's remote to his chest. "We have a job to finish here, Randall," Finn says. He looks to the line of eggs on the ground. "Chase and Ava are going to place this  egg where it belongs. I'll give you back your remote when their job is done. If you try to stop them, I'll either leave you here or send you somewhere far less pleasant."

Randall's face darkens. He must know he only has one choice. "Fine," Randall snaps, plopping down on a rock and crossing his arms. "I'm tired of chasing time jumpers."

Chase and Ava high-five. Finn smiles and tucks the remote into his pocket. One by one, the brontosauruses are returning.

"You have to hurry!" Finn says. Ava and Chase run toward the line of eggs, weaving around the brontosauruses.

CRACK! CRACK! CRACK! The eggs on the ground are all starting to hatch!

Together Chase and Ava quickly place their egg in the one empty spot.

They wait to feel that sense of time stretching and snapping back into place that they've felt each time they've completed a mission. But nothing happens.

The dinosaur mom eyes them angrily. She takes one step toward the line of eggs, then lifts her other leg until it's directly over the egg.

Chase and Ava gasp.

Finn shouts, "NO!"

Even Randall springs up off his rock.

The brontosaurus is going to squash her egg and there's no way to stop her!

A Dino Is Born

The dinosaur's huge foot is now directly on top of the egg! Chase squeezes his eyes closed, afraid to watch. Then he hears what can only be described as a joyful grunt coming from the mom.

"Look, Chase!" Ava shouts. Chase opens his eyes to see the mom gently rolling the egg under her foot. She's not trying to squash it! She's helping it hatch!

CRACK! CRACK! CRACK!

The eggshell begins to split open.
A tiny face pokes out!
The mom nuzzles the
hatching egg. A tiny
leg comes out,
then another.

"This is amazing," Finn says, wiping his eyes. "We're getting to see something no human has seen before."

Chase reaches up to touch the picture of the dinosaur on his baseball cap. He knows how Finn feels. Soon they'll be leaving prehistoric times and this baby dinosaur far behind. But because of what they did, this dinosaur will grow up and then one day thousands of people will get to see him in the museum.

The baby dino must have rolled into the right spot because both remotes begin to buzz. Chase pulls his out, and Finn does the same. Both red buttons are flashing.

Randall reaches out his hand. "Can I have my remote back now?"

Finn seems unsure. "If I give it to you, where are you going to go?"

"Now that I've failed to stop you yet again, I'm going to have to go somewhere my boss can't find me," Randall replies.

"*You have a boss*?" the three of them say at once.

Randall picks up his bag. "Well, I *did*. As of right now, I officially quit stealing things from history. The Collector isn't going to like it."

"Someone named 'the Collector' is behind all this?" Finn asks.

Randall plucks the remote from Finn's hand without answering. He quickly presses the button. "Good luck, time jumpers. I hope to never see you again." He tosses Finn's employee badge at him. "Guess you'll be needing this back."

And with those final words, Randall disappears.